30130505425450

D0185540

Tips for Reading Together

Children learn best when reading is fun.

- Talk about the title and the pictures on the cover.
- Look through the pictures together so your child can see what the story is about.
- Read the story to your child, placing your finger under the words as you read.
- Have fun finding the hidden birds.
- Read the story again and encourage your child to join in.
- Give lots of praise as your child reads with you.

Children enjoy reading stories again and again.
This helps to build their confidence.

Have fun!

Find the bird hidden in every picture.

Silly
Races

Written by Roderick Hunt
Illustrated by Alex Brychta

OXFORD
UNIVERSITY PRESS

Kipper ran.

Kipper got a banana.

Mum ran.

She got an apple.

Biff and Chip ran.

They got an orange.

Dad ran.

Floppy ran.

Oh no! Dad fell.

Dad got a duck!

Think about the story

Why are they silly races?

Which race do you think is the funniest?

Which of the races would you like to be in?

What other sorts of races do people do?

Spot the difference

Find the 5 differences in the two paddling pools.

Useful common words repeated in this story and other books at Level 1.

a   an   got   ran

Names in this story: Mum   Dad   Biff   Chip   Kipper   Floppy